I KNOW AN OLD LADY
WHO SWALLOWED A DREIDEL

A DREIDEL

BY **CARYN YACOWITZ**

ILLUSTRATED BY **DAVID SLONIM**

ARTHUR A. LEVINE BOOKS

AN IMPRINT OF SCHOLASTIC INC.

I know an old lady who swallowed a dreidel,

A Chanukah dreidel she thought was a bagel....

Perhaps it's fatal.

I know an old lady who swallowed some oil—

A pitcher of oil, 'bout ready to boil.

She swallowed the oil to wash down the dreidel,

A Chanukah dreidel she thought was a bagel. . . .

Perhaps it's fatal.

I know an old lady who swallowed some latkes—

Five platters of latkes, hot from the pot-kes!

She swallowed the latkes to fry in the oil

That bubbled and tumbled, 'bout ready to boil.

She swallowed the oil to wash down the dreidel,

A Chanukah dreidel she thought was a bagel. . . .

Perhaps it's fatal.

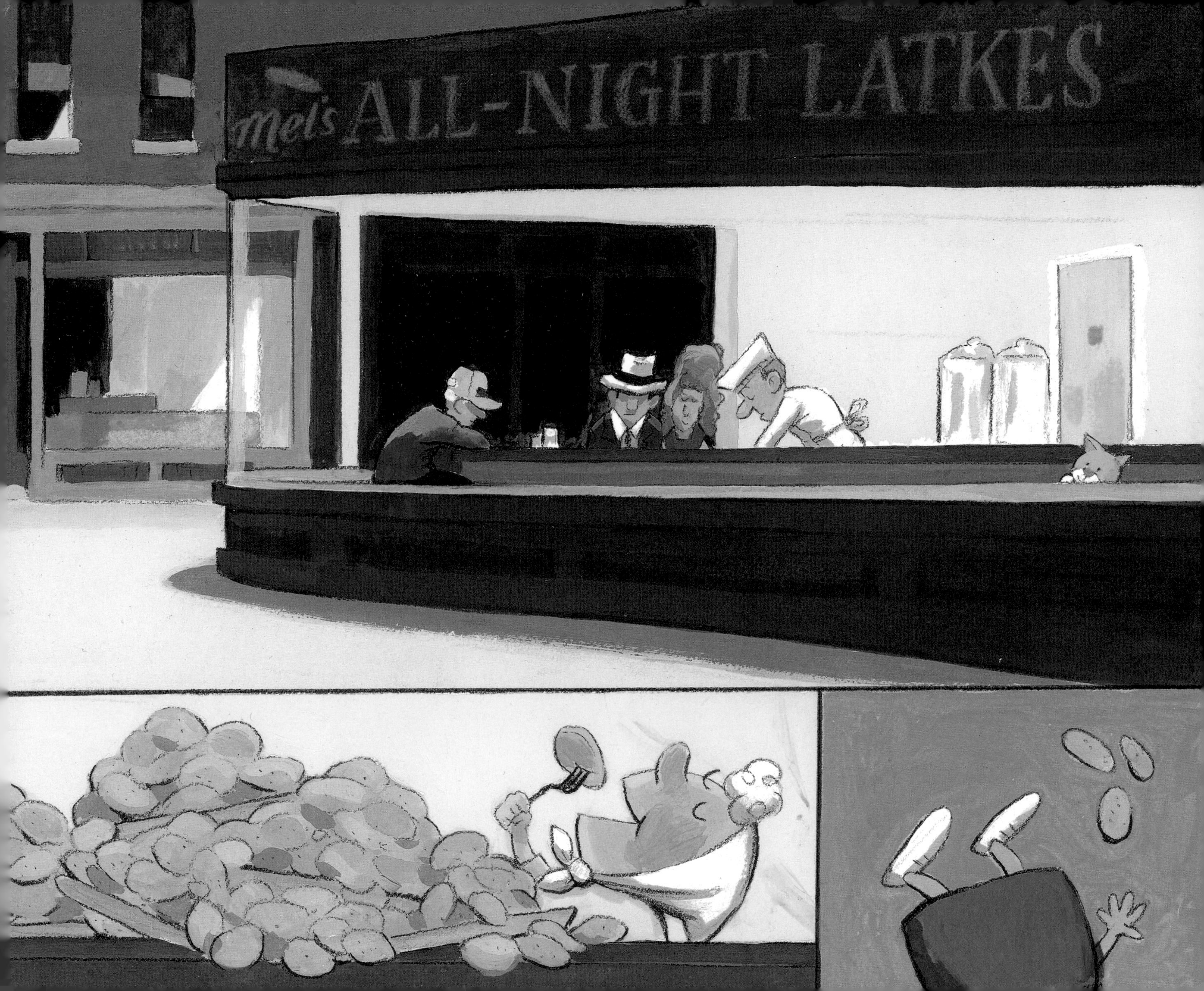
Mel's ALL-NIGHT LATKES

I know an old lady who swallowed some sauce,

Some smooth applesauce that she downed in a toss.

She swallowed the sauce to sweeten the latkes.

She swallowed the latkes to fry in the oil

That bubbled and tumbled, 'bout ready to boil.

She swallowed the oil to wash down the dreidel,

A Chanukah dreidel she thought was a bagel. . . .

Perhaps it's fatal.

I know an old lady who swallowed a brisket.

A twenty-ton brisket! She thought she could risk it.

She swallowed the brisket to soak in the sauce.

She swallowed the sauce to sweeten the latkes.

She swallowed the latkes to fry in the oil

That bubbled and tumbled, 'bout ready to boil.

She swallowed the oil to wash down the dreidel,

A Chanukah dreidel she thought was a bagel. . . .

Perhaps it's fatal.

I know an old lady who swallowed some gelt—

A mine full of gelt, before it could melt.

She swallowed the gelt to follow the brisket.

She swallowed the brisket to soak in the sauce.

She swallowed the sauce to sweeten the latkes.

She swallowed the latkes to fry in the oil

That bubbled and tumbled, 'bout ready to boil.

She swallowed the oil to wash down the dreidel,

A Chanukah dreidel she thought was a bagel. . . .

Perhaps it's fatal.

I know an old lady who swallowed a menorah—

A mountainous menorah, while we danced the hora.

She swallowed the menorah that stood near the gelt.

She swallowed the gelt to follow the brisket.

She swallowed the brisket to soak in the sauce.

She swallowed the sauce to sweeten the latkes.

She swallowed the latkes to fry in the oil

That bubbled and tumbled, 'bout ready to boil.

She swallowed the oil to wash down the dreidel,

A Chanukah dreidel she thought was a bagel. . . .

Perhaps it's fatal.

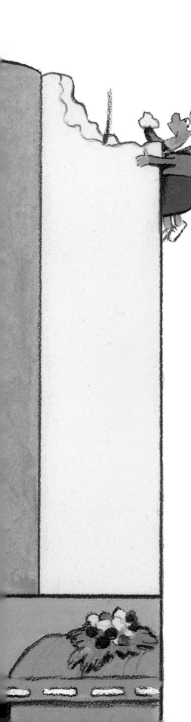

I know an old lady who swallowed some candles.

Eight skyscraping candles were all she could handle!

She swallowed the candles

    That lit the menorah

    That stood near the gelt

    That followed the brisket

    That soaked in the sauce

    That sweetened the latkes

    That fried in the oil

    That washed down the dreidel,

    A Chanukah dreidel she thought was a bagel.

BURP!

PERHAPS . . .

IT WASN'T FATAL!

ARTIST'S NOTE

I hope you enjoyed this romp through art history as much as I enjoyed painting it for you. In these illustrations, I wanted to transform classic works of art not simply to pay homage to paintings and sculptures I love, nor merely to connect the traditional "high culture" of fine art with the popular culture of a folk song and the folk-art style. Most of all, I wanted the art parodies to help the book transcend Chanukah, speaking to the universal human experience of family gatherings and celebrations. Because great art emphasizes what we all have in common, a new look at famous works of art seemed like the perfect way to help people of all backgrounds enjoy this fresh take on an ancient holiday.

Would you like to see each masterpiece my parodies are based on? Here is some information to help you find and appreciate the real things. You can also see links to the works and learn more about my approach to the art at http://www.davidslonim.com/childrens-books/old-lady.

— David Slonim

Mona Lisa (La Giaconda)
1503–1506
Leonardo da Vinci
Musée de Louvre
Paris, France

The Anatomy Lesson of Dr. Nicolaes Tulp
1632
Rembrandt van Rijn
The Royal Picture Gallery Mauritshuis
The Hague, Netherlands

American Gothic
1930
Grant Wood
The Art Institute of Chicago
Chicago, Illinois

The Milkmaid
1660
Johannes Vermeer
Rijksmuseum
Amsterdam, Netherlands

The Scream
1893
Edvard Munch
Nasjonalmuseet
Oslo, Norway

Nighthawks
1942
Edward Hopper
The Art Institute of Chicago
Chicago, Illinois

Campbell's Soup Cans
1962
Andy Warhol
The Museum of Modern Art
New York, New York

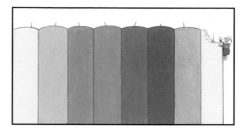

Spectrum II
1966–1967
Ellsworth Kelly
Saint Louis Art Museum
St. Louis, Missouri

*Arrangement in Grey and
Black No. 1 (Whistler's Mother)*
1871
James Abbott McNeill Whistler
Musée d'Orsay
Paris, France

The Thinker
1903
Auguste Rodin
Musée Rodin
Paris, France

Doctor and Doll
1929
Norman Rockwell
Norman Rockwell Museum
Stockbridge, Massachusetts

Christina's World
1948
Andrew Wyeth
The Museum of Modern Art
New York, New York

The Starry Night
1889
Vincent van Gogh
The Museum of Modern Art
New York, New York

Dance (I)
1909
Henri Matisse
The Museum of Modern Art
New York, New York

To my precious granddaughter, Isabel — C. Y.

For Celia — D. S.

Library of Congress Cataloging-in-Publication Data

Yacowitz, Caryn, author.
I know an old lady who swallowed a dreidel / by Caryn Yacowitz; illustrated by David Slonim.   p.   cm.
1. Folk songs, English — Texts. [1. Folk songs. 2. Nonsense verses.
3. Hanukkah.] I. Slonim, David, illustrator. II. Title.
PZ8.3.Y26Iak 2014   782.42 — dc23 2013039437
ISBN 978-0-439-91530-4
10 9 8 7 6 5 4 3 2 1   14 15 16 17 18
Printed in Malaysia 108   First edition, September 2014

The text was set in Adobe Caslon Pro.
The display was set in Bernard MT Condensed Regular.
The artwork was created with acrylic, charcoal, pencil,
and ball-point pen on illustration board.
Book design by David Slonim and Marijka Kostiw